Praise for
The Collection Plate

"Gospel traditions, erotic need, African American–vernacular English, and plenty of blank space on well-organized pages. . . . Allen excels—like Clifton, like Robert Burns—as she shifts into and out of standard English."
—*New York Times Book Review*

"*The Collection Plate* introduces Kendra Allen as a poet to watch. . . . Allen shines a light on the spaces that connect and divide us, coalescing into an electric portrait of joy and pain."
—*Time*

"Kendra Allen's poems examine how religion and hierarchy inform the spaces Black women and girls inhabit—and how we blow past those boundaries, swimming toward the horizon even as the undertow threatens to pull us in another direction."
—*Essence*

"A spectacular debut poetry collection . . . marks the arrival of a singular new talent, a poet whose lyricism is artfully matched by the depths of the emotions she conveys. Allen's poems explore themes of Blackness, womanhood, sex, desire, pain, and belonging, offering glimpses of the casual cruelty and sublime beauty that swim just under the surface of all our experiences."
—Refinery29

"Allen not only vividly captures the experiences of growing up in a Black religious family in the South, transporting readers through specific childhood memories and beautiful tributes, but also provides powerful cultural commentaries. Recommended for all collections."
—*Library Journal*

"*The Collection Plate* is as close as we can get to those looming Black spaces beyond and before language. A book shouldn't be able to do this, but Kendra Allen is a conjurer as much as she is one of the most complete writers we have ever read."

—Kiese Laymon, author of *Heavy* and *Long Division*

"Award-winning essayist Kendra Allen's first poetry collection, *The Collection Plate*, is formally and linguistically invigorating, intertwining and juxtaposing personal and cultural histories to take the reader on a vivid emotional exploration. Allen considers Black exploitation, water crises, white feminism, and the notion of equality among other failures in and of America, reminding the reader of the function of poetry as a form of critique. The speaker's challenging view of God, 'Our Father,' whose contradictions and failures manifest in human men, threads through her relationships with the mother, grandmother, death, and sex, masterfully and inventively orchestrating tension throughout the pages. Though Our Father looms or lurks in the corners of many poems throughout, Allen's bold language demonstrates that she is in command of Our Father's and other deadly forces' presence in her narratives, which she often wields with searing humor. This is a valuable offering; *The Collection Plate* brings to light the dismantling capacity of laughing in the face of power while directly examining it with eyes fired open."

—Emily Jungmin Yoon, author of *A Cruelty Special to Our Species*

"These poems blend personal narrative with social commentary to explore the joy, pain, and underrepresented voices of Black womanhood in America. It's a passionate, fresh, and deeply Southern collection that introduces a new voice you won't want to miss."

—Book Riot

THE COLLECTION PLATE

ALSO BY KENDRA ALLEN

When You Learn the Alphabet

THE COLLECTION PLATE

Poems

Kendra Allen

ecco

An Imprint of HarperCollinsPublishers

HarperCollins books may be purchased for educational, business, or sales promotional use. For information, please email the Special Markets Department at SPsales@harpercollins.com.

Ecco® and HarperCollins® are trademarks of HarperCollins Publishers.

A hardcover edition of this book was published in 2021 by Ecco, an imprint of HarperCollins Publishers.

FIRST ECCO PAPERBACK EDITION PUBLISHED 2022

Designed by Michelle Crowe

Background Image by Kyrylo/Adobe Stock

Library of Congress Cataloging-in-Publication Data has been applied for.

ISBN 978-0-06-304848-5 (pbk.)

22 23 24 25 26   LSC   10 9 8 7 6 5 4 3 2 1

For my mouth
and the water
for the mirrors
and the rope
what a waste

"I feel numb in this kingdom."

—Daughter

"Crawl to the altar
pride won't let me walk."

—theMIND

Contents

THE COLLECTION PLATE

Evening service

when it's time for the invitation, we say Our Father
today is a blessed one   walk to the front of the altar
in my pretty printed please you dress
socks with the ruffles at the ankle ready
to give this life over or never see eternity
I sit in   the chair and the pastor thanks mama for her persuasion
the pastor is our uncle and our uncle tells me   in two weeks imma be saved
                                     in two weeks this a renew
                        -ed discipline
but still he's so stingy   this impatience for assurance   leads me back
they get me ready in my come let us adore him   mama tell me to take off
     my panties   she forgot   to bring extra types of loss
                 at set time I walk out from behind
     the choir stands   the curtains open   the people scream
there's dead water bugs wrapped round fallen leaves from no sky
in the tub I'm in   my uncle recites a scripture so it don't look like we live here
for the good show
I watch them congregate   over the sinning as water rushes   down the amen
     my feet
panicked cause they can't touch
     an end   I envision modeled men   his hand holding
nostrils   my mouth miracled   if I could sing this wouldn't be loveless

if I could swim I wouldn't die

the pastor is our uncle and our uncle holds me under at a distance

the pastor is our uncle and our uncle divests me of my volition

back on land   I drip

I dribble, I cough up

who I shoulda been   the people clap at how clean, how quickly my design has ripped

their wants   an encore—for me to swallow it better   hold it all in

longer

say sorry for wasting   my first eight years of life

Look at the material
after Tiffany Pollard

Put it in
Somebody

's mouth:

I was never a child

as soon as I popped out
I was just
in the know
intact
only because I slept

and if I ever make
myself

a mummy
or a mommy

I just wanna say I'm back
and I look better
backed into

I'm the queen bitch
up in here

and I love Our Father

I only left
over my ambiguities

I was choked up

were you trying?

I'm not the type
to hold
some shit
in

I'll smear it

face down

just cause it applies
I ask
the questions
which pockets to dump
into

I don't know nothing well
but I know
it's big

if it's about
my mouth

my language

or lip stain

I'm the note held toward the end

of "Inside My Love"
U know, when she's vanishing

       To think, one woman made two
       complete things in me bout loving, bout laying   yet I still don't
       know the difference between pleasure and penetration
       or what to do with my hands in the middle of
  the kindest insertions

       it ain't enough   ringing possible   to let go
                   turn into glitter,   into powder—here's to well rounded
wound
turn that sad shit up

Minnie swear it's tranquil
to be permitted
or water a holed nation
with just the tip

I was only seven

if I can remember it
right   I know
if it won't fit, to hold it

inside

      all five fingers

          & squeeze

Company is coming over

                you hurt
in my coffin
can feel it, the creaking

you say I grind
my teeth at night   but you never open my mouth

                           see the back row
                           begging

                           for a changeling
                           some sloped hells

                           when you lay
                           can you hear

                           our gifts
                           you made into a release,   a fist

                           -ful of it wrapped up
                           in skin——a stress ball
          petitioning

to be ransom   that way,
a family name can mean something

that way we can share
the same death bed

that way I work for cheap
and light our flame   and lean into leniency

and request to forget mornings

Solace by earl

"I got my Grandmama's hands
I start to cry when I see 'em, 'cause they remind me of seeing her."

—Earl Sweatshirt

I speak to Grandmother
and she opens up
the screen door
Hands so heavy if they ever came down on me,   I would disperse
Hallucinate, or die   like the cacti in her yard   like she did
'nt redistribute them hands
them feets   [same way]   them knuckles knotted, I swear I caught a body, a ghost
wouldn't bleed us through like that, like pillars of the house that cracked
the cement running down her cheeks   I skip over
them all, stomp yards toward yellow panels yellow toe stumps
be curving like lust—   slanted,   baby, is you knocked knee'd? Done fell out
of sandals by the time the steeple show
I sit on the floor
boards with a heater blowing
in fall against my khakis
where we rerun *everybody loves raymond*
and I'm the closest great-grandchild
Before she drifts   I say I rather deepen

out into back streets   I got stories
Say I be scared to talk over there but really she's so tall
It's always shit I got to practice toward turning into
                    —A stand in Grandmother
                    's house in the fate of my name
                    ain't got no letters no more and my name
                    is one of the last names
                    I hardly remember the sound of her mumbling
                          Staring into that droopy mouth
                              Eagle eying the twist of her tongue
                        Scouting what made her
                go
its majesty the only reason I can commit
to the numbness. My after-school harbor
my boat to trembling descent.

I see Grandmother on weekends now
I picture her fingers grabbing at marrow,
Digging her dynasty out of me so she can save it
for when she's missing out. I picture her in the recliner,
Burying what she mined into a photo album. When really she sits
straight up don't even ask
where I been

If I'm not my mother

He won't mention love soon
My remorse, coming
   This man my nothing
Thighs upward,   arranged like exiting a good life
Hallucinating bodies behind mine   pressing
   sprouting a functioning in the fold
      Thinkin   why am I not a forgiver
& years later wonder why I'm deserted
   without an eating of breath,   the ease
My bottom will open up   for isolated men

The invention of the Super Sadness! was an accident

show me how to make fun things

or happy accidents   How to open up sis

's dolls, see how she blinks   without a life

line. If I'm little, show me how to win

games and become a burned boy

who's present   enough   to keep standing

in doorways without shoving   show me

my name and its prototype. Let me craft elastic;   let me

be better   even with the fear

of water   even when

I'm sent into planets to build bombs to keep bombs from obliterating

these burdens

show me how to shoot these niggas faster, fill up

tubs, carry space

packs, become fire

that holds silly knuckles

Show me the crack at my head   recede   from the filthy state

waters of fifty wet states. Wave. Wave.

Make me

artless   Make me

barren

I hate when niggas die

Times of death&
Suddenly, women need hugs
They all becoming—something,   winged
tipped—or just pretty girls,   maybe
We all become pretty
girls in the face
Of man if caskets fit
Sharp lines penciled in   the aesthetic
of Our Father's cadavers   nature boys
& we breathe fine
What else are our torsos   for
strong-armed into surrender
Umbilicaled into figure eights

& no boundaries for the spine

Our Father's house (i)

Remind it I'm a rattletrap
nausea in my kinship

#FreeMyNiggas but free my niggas

I put hands on myself
close the deal of lemme hold a dolla
       outta my classics
cymbal it all back
       in my palm, the turnaround
       rate immaculate

       an enforcement

a penchant of what currency cohabits

the causality of we was little and never scolded each other
       's needs   now the missing in life, in age
       feels violent

              time gets cut short no matter what

              Guess who got locked up?
              Who?
              Guess.
              Who? {is a placeholder}
              GUESS!!!

It's funny how instinctual ya name is—the way it comes tumbling off the tongue—the way I caress the syllables of it, might as well had séanced *eons* the way we get enormous

The way we cultivate an offense before we get to fractions—the way you get out and stay in all at once—the way you still owe me a dolla—the way pride both ways get us fucked up—the way you go back a month later—the way a month after that she get killed and all of us are forgotten freedom flags

Ain't no rallies—ain't no protests—ain't no local night news bout a ghetto girl head wound with three babies at home and a daddy on his second strike

It winds us, the weight of hoping
you know you got wings and a brain and a name and words and
patience for a payback too but lately it's like

> *Guess who died?*
> *Who?*
> *Guess?*
> *I don't know!!*
> *You.*

A trilogy everyone watches

At first I thought throwing
out the junk would humble me
that a baby being born
        would be enough
        for folk to drop,
      calm   into the flat line
that the only thing I would want is
something constant: they always go   in threes
cast in a trilogy everyone watches   like a banging
against my ear after the chin check, or a fellowship of trees
to cleanse me the glass
        shards inside of baby breaths
        lining it like a collar in my sleep
        the five births since our last showing
   I eat a couple, thinking I can meet me
     taste buds be elevating   done hopped into the imaginary
liquid living in the belly like my name Jonah
    memory be divorcing itself like Our Father did
       in the beginning
       yet we still prepare   dinner for a denomination
   just to stress

out the street lights
      shrink back into summers
ain't no need to sorrow   the sticky
          stuff
when kids gotta learn to grieve   too

My sex wet

Who saw the sticky tie itself
To my navel

My hair the color of damp sand now
Because I made it that way

Lethargic, because I was made   that way
Forcep baby, forced into my life

Trying constantly to omit myself back
Into the body

My sex wet
In Mama's gut
Because, yes.

Not sure if I wanted to be here
Now I change cities every couple of years

It's a cessation whenever I'm touched

I come to you as humbly as I know how

                    I wonder
               is this worship supposed to make me
                    want
                    to say a different prayer
               sound out these syllables into a synagogue
oh, I know
what to capsize   once I stop   the nightly leaning
all this bending this waking   blasphemous
                    not to god
               but to most mothers
                    who are
                    my god   I swear
               the only thing I spray without stem
is thank you   Father   for this mother—   for this   you are almighty
wonderful and all knowing
          I think
that's how she phrases it every time she auditions   for your love
          I realize
all gold is just   a chain
a menagerie of sorts
and other words I can't pronounce
like I come to you
as humbly

as I know how   which is really just worth ecclesiastical jest   or my uncle
's mistress
         I don't think   the markings of missionary   gets enough
credit
for what it procreates
         oh, I mean
no disrespect   but if I sit on it   I'd just write
things they told us
you said   never take   recognition for your miracles   which means your tongue
has been a mirage
         I sink
         during all sermons
         I figure   the point is:
all mamas pray   and   Our Father, which   never stops   saying sorry
oh, I reckon   Father
it was compulsion   to absolve men
         I auction   all ceremonies
for facts
for I know   realistically,   most mothers of sons
         must go

The many times I failed to defend my mother to Our Father

I think this death will be like the ones in the
movies
where the brunt
is shot out of me and I bleed on the inside   & nothing
falls
out, so it feels more urgent
the yellow tape
the sunflower warnings
the sexed loins
the child's pose
express for three
laned collisions
the only exception
when I'm home
curled up in an integrated intimacy
                    in revered galaxies
my leg wrapped around them all   like I'm the best husband   for convincing
        I stroke the holy   act out of love
                        I mean today
                when I tried it, it became a vocation
            each layer a laceration

I mean, at least today
I've never been without
a grace period   a life
sentence
at least a smear of closure

We had died real quick

                    the point is
we knew we   for drowning
couldn't swim   forgive, ourselves
the discharge   into shared customs
from our buried   for our buried
told us so   break into the surf
the tightening inside   routine into repentance
our ribs, told us no   wring a woman out
the sirens in the air   dragged into a fasting
warned us first   a sayer, a vacancy
the buoyed bristle   walk on its border
turned—left   tone our limbs
lungs circumstantial   atone our sins
then waves crashed   crash the wave

Learning to tread water

Breathing I learned
is fully mechanical. Created
for wide scale treasure
hunt. A scam to have to descend
hundreds of feet I sat my dumbass in the midst of it all
Deep underwater, my breathing is still suspect. And deep underwater breathing even
underwater, they've never called us an us or even silver and gold. That's how I learned
everything I is   been buried.

At camp, the sickle
celled children love
the hour they have to spend
in the pool everyday

you'd think their lives didn't
depend on immersion

like they don't have enough
of nothing   when saviors jump in

say   *hood kids can't swim*
and   *it's a shame but thank you*
for   *allowing us to teach them*

they don't say there ain't enough
pools to be found in Galilee anyway

or that these kids can be found

dead at the bottom of any body
of water whether they can swim or not

smaller salvations give them
lessons and they get better, graduate
to red wristbands and learn how to jump
in the deep end without holding
their noses, they say no breath

holding games, but we practice with ours

first, we show them how to handle
their bodies stiff
on top of the water;   play dead

then we show them what to do when they need

to sink.

Collection plates

Sunday

mornings. The church
pastor will imply
we—
[not] meaning him
are all addicted to pardoning
shit that should be financed

a sanctification that two-steps
in between the art
-eries and thumbprint

wound: apparent

climbing and
jumping

wound: makes you
prophetic

strapping string into
the fallible

wound: buys you land

laid out and
threatening to time

the gentle out of limitation
stuck in its solo

knowing that there
is more than an instant

wound: forthcoming

Our Father's house (ii)

Father, are you feeding me?
Father, look at me!
Father, look at me!
Father, hold these guts right quick!
so I can snatch my brain's body back
Father, you know
I'm an auditory lova

All the things that stretch out my lower back

When my sky fell all I asked for was gold teeth

I swear I saw mouths strained   singing choruses
after the front yard's organs   cut out its center

        hallelujah hallelujah   three-part harmony

striking pavement like my Father

's Nature was
just a next-door neighbor

  if the bite bounced off and pilgrimaged,

is this not destruction?

        my gap guilted

into reshaping the earth

       into every man   I would never love

is this not the existence of the new world in my womb
-less grip?

my happy baby full and proud

my rope chewed out

washing itself down with wishing well

                phenotype: expansive

                    nose, thick

                    -hipped
                knuckles tight as desert
                -ed throats

    a god

who is most

  of us   &them

at once

        where we circle

      confines til'

                        all suns go down
where we realign in intervals where it's us and not me, again

won't slide right out
can't make no plans

when you a constellation

I hear layers are what keeps you

warmest

Naked & afraid

One of the biggest challenges contestants face
on the show is finding drinkable water. Out in
deserts and forests, they strip down with only
machetes and mosquito nets for protection against
the wild unknown. The real survivalists, they bring
pots. If they're lucky, they set up shelter by an open
stream, stay close to water and stay alive. If unlucky,
they dig for traction from a tree trunk where it takes
its time finding frequency. In both cases, water must
be boiled or your insides crumble. Dirty water rips
through the surface for twenty-one days. It's no way
to water test a script.

When contestants without pots
get desperate, they drink straight
from the source. This last hope
results in projectile vomiting into
fallen tree trunks, excreting
diarrhea in front of millions of
watchers, and in extreme cases
having to be evacuated from
the show. Drinking from
contaminated waters leads to
intestinal infection, E. coli, lead

poisoning, parasites, pesticides
and pathogens. Now quiet bodies
fill themselves with impurities. Everyone
knows you can't drink bad water.
When waters are wrong, they might
as well swallow spit. Their bodies
shrinking to unnatural smallness,
but ain't this all the things we was
told would make us, better.
to watch them die   when we know
there's always enough
clean water near
       by

Afraid & naked

One of the biggest challenges citizens face
is finding drinkable water. Out in
streets and kitchens, they strip down with only
plastic bottles and sewers for protection against
the wilderness of government sanctions. The real
survivalists (all of them) have mastered the use
of a pot. If lucky, they bathe themselves in home
-town tubs that night. If unlucky, they don't
bathe at all. In both cases, water must be boiled
or your insides crumble. Dirty water guts them
from the inside out for five years. It's no way
to water test a system.
When citizens without pots
get thirsty, they don't have
options. This American way
results in bodies of children,
a news story, and in extreme
cases, residents plead for
showmanship then evaporate.
Drinking from contaminated
waters leads to Legionnaires'
disease, lethal pneumonia,
abandonment, dehydration,

paranoia. Now quiet bodies fill
themselves with impurities.
Everyone knows you can't
drink bad water. When waters
are wrong, we've failed
their survival. Their bodies shrinking
like their population,
but ain't this all the things
we was told would make us, better.
to watch them die   when we know
there's always enough
clean water near
    by

The water cycle

In Miss Lady's science class, she compromises the water
cycle but none of us can stop

Staring at her ass. The thong in her crack slacks around
the waist which, always leaves, that lil opening where we

Bloom. *The water cycle*, she sings. Manipulating moods for us
to remember what will be on the weekly test.

Everybody knows she's a singer interrupted by a coastline.
The water cycle. Because of her we now know endowment's lull.

ECP—it repeats itself. It brings down raaaaain. Sleet, snow, or hail.
Evaporation, Miss Lady says, is when your chest becomes hollow.

Condensation is when the ticker cracks and your eyes swell
from the pressure. Precipitation is when Our Father calls a caveat, a home.

Practical life skills

We pull up to the dock with three picnic chairs as crickets chirp
Sit close to water   on wood till sunrise   I tell fish
To hush, quiet down so I can hear about hydrated hierarchies
Not fins flapping to remain wet   I tell you it's like they know

What's about to happen You hand me the pole the
Automatic one for my child hand barely balmed
One push of a button, I learn how to secure shrimp round
The hook this is our Father / daughter dance I hook and hook

Make sure those shrimp are safe & dead when they hit salt's loophole   repeat
Until no more are in the bucket, cause worms ain't never gone
Get me nothing worth   cooking up We came out here for a reason
Not to pretend we enjoy each other's company I watch fish hop round

In dark matter water and wonder what it would be like to live away from
A cliff   then You catch a blowfish and bang its head up against the concrete
On top of the dock we watch it die You didn't have to kill it
You throw it in an empty cooler   we continue hooking   I share all your names

Melatonin

if everyone in the world could fall

        asleep no longer   it means:
                                       i failed my Grandmother;
                                       my god

body defining this as foresight; meticulous matter

        when eyes close & nothing
     is said for the way it melts   how is it any different

than when we become lovers, conquerors   tired   as in unfortunate   as in
congruent

     & we eat the limbs now

when at first it was just the nails

Our Father's house (iii)

It's all the same thing

It's a villainous love

Been back before

It's one of my proverbial memories   the cleaved grunting
Notorious, because I don't know what to do   with my lips

Really I could crochet them   Grandmothers teaching me to go
In and back around before I dredge

      Loose clothing—a misuse, a slip-
Up. My hips parabled to picture pressure   stiff & bloodless

Fine-toothed, ready   to either cut or sharpen when I close
the door, it means we prescribed a cure

Made something   fit
   &I got free

Range without intervention.
This is either finna make sense

or we gone break

The Super Sadness! feels like anger which feels like

Foreskin. A default setting.
midnight. Dry eyes.
Hesitation at an intersection.
Premature adulthood.
sheets. Freelancing. Yes maybe.
knuckles. Hypervigilance. Corn stubs
between my gap. A sucked-in stomach. Sycning.
        Infantile embroidery. Showtime. The next step.
My pocketbook. Learned behavior.
hand gripping. When my Grandmother was
yesterday but forgot all them years ago. Resolution. Yardsticks. Small talk. An incubator.
Groupthink. A Ferris wheel.
water at the bottom of a three-foot pool. Meaning to swallow water at the bottom
of a three-foot pool. Not drowning. Sex sometimes. Compulsive eating. A fed family.
Liquidated compensation.
walking up a flight of steps.
conditioning. Method acting.
Crashing. An accessory.
I felt better. Staying together.
chafing. Losing my life.
Cotton candy. The end of "Throw Away."

Stomach   churns   after
Sunday   morning   worship.
Changed   passwords.
Missed   deadlines.   Fitted
        Momentum.   Ashy
                stuck   in
        Primary colors.
An exit. Intermediate
        supposed to turn 100
Melodrama. Accidentally swallowing
Weakened   breaths   after
A   glitch.   Controlled   air
A   book   release   party.
Writing what I do & wishing
I'll air all this shit out. Thighs
        Gnats   in   a   kitchen.
        635   heading   to

Mesquite. Mesquite. Light voices. isolation. Everything. Hyphenated. date. My idol in mourning state. Getting to know you. Room temperature out. A fan blowing hot air.

Black exploitation. An Promotion. An expiration An organization. water and the sun is What I always wanted.

Let's leave

Dear dying,
Dear dying,
Dear dying,

I am
I am Dry lipped and chapped
Dry lipped and chapped Call my name

In the light
One

Syllabled
body weighted Depleted of
I wonder what it feels like   until   my body
Moisture

To lose my belly is wrung out, tightly
I could

drink
To be thirsty   to have my so when I'm   aired out   I'm immovable

but I like it
Tongue   when   skin peels
Scraped of its   taste

47

I ain't never baked a thing from scratch a day in my life

Every time
I enter
          I   leaven,
          my   liquids

     so hard I pinch
nerves from five fingers   just go ask

every fallen wall

          if I open back up

          to ask   the ether

             archive all my niggas

       their names & numerals,   their numbed ankles

   just   piece it all together for 'em   please   cater to them
answer when they call

Our Father's house (iv)

                                                    I like to ride
                                                  in Caddys too

                              because of what apostles
               represent

Chihuahuas

Bark cause that's what they supposed to do.

Mouths wide open at all times.

Teeth over chin until you touch them.

This is a story about man.

Low-hanging hazard signs.

Lapped dogged behind wooden fences.

Drifting the land without a permit.

Constantly apologizing for reappearing.

Forget the menses;

It was bad to mercy the union.

The mention of the spread eagle.

I think they're punishing us for punishing us.

We all got lil man complexes.

I'm tired of yo ass always crying

From mountains, they let stones fall   on me _____

all to free

the nipple.   They cry wolf when they are wolves Their tribe

puffy eyes. They cry _____ when nothing hurts

at all. Watch us perish   _____,

_____,

_____.   They lie

then cry _____.

They take

then cry _____.   They offend

then cry _____.   They lose

then cry   from shame that they could ever lose   with those tears.

Never _____ do they really mean wounded   militia. _____ they claim

equality

     in my name   while being treated better

than all of us. _____, for birthright, they're gifted a savior   & still, they will

cry

     if you care for me—and when you hear the sound, believe me   we must run.

a) for fun
a) for sadness
a) for safety
a) for the credit of their liberations

If you throw me in this water what you're telling me is you want me dead

    I thought I loved
that dirty water but
        water, it seems, is the most interesting
thing about you   your river bodying   all that blood
you let flow
           downstream
down south water be moving in coils
      tastes   like coal   our bonfire nights
You even have the nerve to name it black,   a warrior
                  up by the pool house
                  water browns and
                  black ink stains as usual

                  river keepers, pool boys
                  decompose because of it
                  omega keep drowning
                  too early

                    in depths
                  designed specifically for flooding
                  the breaststroke
                  brown water kids scrub fields
                  of concrete in its remembrance
                  wading pools of deceit: a queen

in the city regulates bout grazed
feet touching grounds, it's based
on convenience or life
shields needing armor
to precede everything: brewing companies and councils for places
to store my talent and hoard fish dead enough to fry at the expense of baking
yo ass in the sun
we sit at the pool
'   's sidelines,
a coolant tells us

when the shower water hits me back,
it's harsh, i never feel clean
i don't open my mouth when it rains
niggas know how to do everything   but stay
above it
but bet i won't
get my hair wet

Most calvaries have dead people

"white men offer more protection to their prostitutes than
black men offer to their best women"

—nannie helen burroughs

like Our Father
        when he gives me his issues
places them in my spine   lets me,

        sew skin into skin without thread

and tells me to walk

to a city where i am given something more
        than a man

        whose obligation is to no one, not even
the Blood

if there's dying to be done, we did it
        together   on our own calvary

i musta been dead girl all alone

if I opened

myself

in the middle of a sea, my insides floating   in folded waves
                              yearning for the deep
end

to knock me under

                            if there's hand-holding
i thought the held
      whistles possessed warnings

           to make
complete sentences without a stutter

    the exhalation
overlapping the harness

coming back stouter

taking all of my good
               replacing my good

filling me back up with saltwater

tying me back up in spit
telling me it's my fault
      how could you let me   spill all over town

The maybe memory

1.

lay back on the top corners of an aluminum chair

shoulder blades should be bout wide as the kitchen

2.

sink then scratch all recall from the head that's too big

to support the neck, become newborned again by a shampoo splash

3.

down a white tee. gone have to stop being fraid

of water between the ears one day. sounds of music don't count

4.

& waves & every other word.

head in the sink, slip hands down the shaft of fleece

5.

ducking dampness. if younger, it'll fit, full

bodies could lay where bread is but now it's face down

6.

look inside the drain, scrape

hair out in clunks. the fall out. the maybe memory.

Happy 100th birthday

This
is my first time
at your headstone
& I keep remembering
the day the laws came
to pick me
up from the steps
I told them to take me
to you. Dipped them
into backstreets to get
to the back
of Haas out front.
It's nighttime.
You been sleep.
And cops at yo door
ain't an indication
to wake up. They came
in. You told them bye.
You let me sit in
the dark to cry heavy
to call on Our Father, I'm sure
I forgot this was
a kind of home too.

I'm sure I forgot
this was a kind of
home too as I wipe
mud out of you
-r plot's large intestines.
Like I'm planting
a recall in your back
and you'd remember
one of our names
and you'd become
a baby doll. Re-charging.
If I dug your grave
this is what I'd look like.
Stepping on so many
bodies
to get to yours,
just to find out,
you happy.

To find out you happy
I barely realized
I could miss you
and the Sweet Georgia
Brown plates packed
with mac, cabbage,
& other smothered things
We like to suffocate that way
and suffer that way
That's why we like to stand in
that line on Sundays
and that's why they put you
in a nursing home
let the juice spill, down
your chin
and that's why they let you die
when you couldn't even
say nothing back
all yo history in adult
diapers. All yo history
in rooms with none of you
in it.

All yo history
in rooms with none of you
in it
and I go back
to re-visit it
acknowledge our fabric.
It was a suggestion
but I need you
again—
to write.
I'm sorry nothing comes
before that need
to remember everything.
The house is now
refurbished, remodeled,
better. All the words
we wanted for your brain.
All your stuff sold and
for what
a vacation.
The yellow gone.
Everything in
the garage, gone.
The chair, gone.
And I can see it
all from the window
of my car, the failure.
At least I'm honest
about the things
I care about.

I'm honest
about the things
I care about. I don't feel
nothing sitting out front.
Don't even see you
sitting in the recliner
or salved. You
owned something
then they seized you.
You had the biggest back
yard surrounded by wire,
clotheslined our courtship
now there's a fence bordered
around it. Someone preserved
and took care of what we
couldn't. Not that you would
care, cause you dead and pain
-less. Hopefully   memory   is
keeping
you up at night now. I just want
-ed to make sure you still
the oldest person I know.

Who say good folk ain't supposed to die

I did.

Twice.

When I eulogize Our Father

The reason we have gathered
        here today   is because   I know how it looks
when Our Father loves something
     His Cadillac. His bullets. His garden.   His weed. His tractor. His dogs.
The first time I saw him cry, the damn dog died
and after—he cried every time he saw me   it felt
     like thousands of tears ran into my toes as I watched him collapsed over
a corked mouth   I felt so sorry
     for seeing
each time Our Father's eyes ached for more breath and no bleeding   the way my mouth
mumbled the morning our beasts met   out in the front yard
how his tried to tear the meat
from my paw
     there was a leak   a war
of wrists   I got from riding in that Cadillac casket
         he ashed each handheld thing there   then forgot to show up
    through an open window   the dust landing on my cheek like another tameless thing
I've swallowed oxy and oxygen because of this love
I know it was the blood
I know it was the blood of me
Our Father never offered   no loyalty to the child
only ultimatums of wildflowers or respect—and I decline both   if you ever have to
down a shot of something brown with your maker

it ain't polite

all it ever wants is to see   a mother's hornet   coated against the clear

once, we died off of its clarity   and I danced in front of the tv   barely aware of the bruise

expanding through the tile   we cooked meals there often   it's how the walls

wrapped around Our Father are my teeth—undomesticated,   dense

        lock jawed through entire legacies

eventually,   he just closed his eyes

traditionally, I've always been hard

        to forgive

"No one had told her about the end of love"

from *Sex in the City,* Season 1, Episode 1

when you let someone be
-sides you,
let someone else mend
you, what does that say About
your weakness

Leave me alone

With nothing   but the slurry of an organ
maybe   a lake   to
dip my feet in   money
trees to pick my fruit from
a mini fridge

to keep   it all fresh while

I lie   on my back
threatening to throw   all my stuff   away for good
let it wilt into my body   of water   every better thing
that don't involve ideals
of better things   I'll never have
a sanctuary for

If I am the Father

My bottom will open up   for influential men
    without an eating of breath
& years later I will wonder why I'm deserted
        Thinking   why am I not forgiven
sprouting a family in the fold
Celebrating bodies behind mine   pressing
Thighs upward,   arranged like exiting a good life
    If this man is myself
My remorse ricocheted
Hoping, love is just a word

Birth of black bishop

If ya'll don't do nothing
else,

ya'll a shame

      women

for babies

                    to boost
by candlelight   a drip of oil

                  The pharisaic
                  portrait
                  a payment

                  ya'll anoint
        ya'll selves
        the experiment of exceptionalism or some time
        to miss touch
a flock of fingertips mostly
socketed around earlobes

calling out

all the wrong   names   you wanna be   a shepherd so bad

                  just open the gate   I'm gon put on my robe too

                        tell the story

                                  rejoice in a multitude of voices

                                  hit that note on time

          I won't tell nobody

          the offering was never invested

Our Father's house (v)

Tell Our Father, please

                                    fill me with remnants
                                    of my born one
                                    so finally
                                    we can mourn
                                    one another

Sermon notes

Note: In the night
         nothing rises, tranquility bubbles when the air is off

Note: Find your reflection

Note: A prairie that houses ankles and elbows   fistfight full of shoulders
         leaning into shoulders, pushing for a worshiper

Note: Illuminated conversions when you look in the mirror

Note: You have to love him even if you don't

Note: When you start to fan, senses stimulated,   the door is creaking
         & prayer can't open it

Note: Find your rope

Note: Passion is a kind of florescence   a water well in its rapture
                                    and then you find

      your burning man

Gifting back bread & barren land

If this is reversible
I won't employ my wrist   I'd kneel against my desire
And know what centers all soil is   sealed scarring, or who swings first
Still I respected its balding, I just for-   ge/t names all the time, lately the face
Is punished, or persisting I gape simpler   for intention never fixes iridescent infamy
Salt outlining the spectral who won't drop   its mighty or barricade the stock out of this
Stomach my kind of romance: to give, me   me back. Ideally, I'm still acquainted with ties
Gifting back bread & barren land   's wonder. Outlandish to resist
Goodbye as an optioned flick   a giver's tongue a rapture
If this is a process, no   weight is left to coerce
Only so many ways I can say oh   & sliver out
of it wholly, the doormat   from our fin
-gertips. I touch commencements   stand in moot points
of maybe there ain't no mo' people left to fit in to   our tributes of leasing
I be lying
if I said proximity determined where my darling goes   by my breasts
or by the border—I replicate   I clone   I become
less strained by vacant mouths   like I falsify sound mind in order to risk
evil as infancy—a presentation, or is it
just elegant denial   I always been a better
writer than a figure   folk be carrying
transcripts for a full exit   but I be leaving   all my clothes—rid myself   a
relinquished
lashing
where nothing is lined   up   no hanger
no bell

Acknowledgments

One time after my great-grandmother let me and my cousins count quarters on the floor of her yellow house, we thought we was rich. Mama took all of us to Sonic because Grandmother wanted to get out the house and liked them nasty burgers, so she balled out on all of us. We got whatever we wanted. Chili dogs. Cream slushes. Lemon-berry slushes mixed with peach. Burgers. Just going crazy on the menu. Got anything we wanted that whole day. Then as we pulled up into Grandmother's driveway to drop her back off, my Mama turned around, looked at us all in the backseat—probably ready to ask for something else, and said, noun one of ya'll said thank you all day. She ain't sound mad about it, she just reminded us whether you're deserving or not, people do things out the kindness of they heart, not because they got to. Then she started talking bout how we could've offered to use some of the money we just got to get what we wanted, but I definitely stopped listening by then. This story is way longer, but just know I never forgot to say thank you again. I think about that moment all the time, so grateful for it. Thankful for getting to spend the time I did with my great-grandmother Etta G. Smith. Tall woman.

Cactus owner.

Haas St. legend.

First woman I saw be mean and not care; and this somehow feels most important to me. Thank you for all the silence, Coca-Colas, and Blue Bell Homemade Vanilla. Still the oldest person I've ever known.

Thank you to L. Lamar Wilson, whose words changed the direction of this collection. You told me these poems needed to be "put in somebody's mouth," and

I spent a year putting them in Our Father's. Thank you for your eyes, your poetry, general love for Us, and giving this book a voice to follow; you were its first reader.

Marya, thank you for checking in with me even when you weren't my agent, for being honest with me about this business once you became my agent, and for being the best and always looking ahead.

Mr. Daniel Halpern, who believed in me with an immediacy that was jarring. Shout-out to our mutual love of line breaks. You gave me so many encouraging words. Thank you so much, nothing but respect.

Gabriella, Sonya, and everyone at Ecco for answering whatever question or concern I had and all the hard work. Thank ya'll.

Thank you to *december* and *The Paris Review*, which published versions of some of these poems.

To everybody in the Documentary Poetics course at UA who workshopped versions of most of the water poems, thank ya'll for the guidance.

To every single student in my fall 2019 Intro to Creative Writing class, thank ya'll a whole lot. I promise I learned more.

Nabi and Sarah and Aurielle and Zoe, thank ya'll for having me and literally being an example of what healthy love and community look like. Ya'll are the brilliant, beautiful, talented, fearless humans I hope to become. I feel better just knowing ya'll. Alisha, thanks for our talks that last hours but don't feel like it. Thank you, Nana, for making sure I know I'm still family and Bria for fighting and being my best friend. Josh for spending a year and a half listening to me talk in circles of confusion and still telling me I got it all under control when it was clear I had none, big thank you. And big shout-out to my weighted blanket cause where would I be without my BABY. Shout-out to me for taking my time, finally.

So much gratitude to all the bodies of work that helped me create this body of work. This book wouldn't have happened at all if I didn't bury myself in Boogie's *Everythings for Sale* almost every day. Sometimes multiple times a day. Not only is it the type of art I wanna make, but it got me through the year of 2019. Jean Deaux's *Empathy* EP, Jamila Woods's *LEGACY! LEGACY!*, and Etta Bond's *He's Mine*—like c'mon now, master classes that were constantly in rotation. The movie *Waves*. Fred Hammond's *Somethin' 'Bout Love*. Jessie Reyez's pen in general. Tinashe's *Nightride*. Whoever in Arcade Fire that wrote "Sometimes I can't believe it / I'm moving past the feeling again." "Inside My Love" by Minnie Riperton. Season 1 of *David Makes Man*. Daughter's *Not to Disappear*. "Solace" by Earl Sweatshirt, always and forever. "Can't Handle the Truth" by JoJo. Smino's *Noir*, Masego's *Lady Lady*, and Banks's *The Altar*. Jaden Smith's "B," "L," "U," "E," which, not even being dramatic, changed my life. Brandy's *Afrodisiac*. "What Is This" by Mary Mary and "Life" by Big K.R.I.T.

Thank you to anybody who said my name in a room I wasn't in or went out their way to connect me or offer advice, preciate cha'! Thank you to all Our Fathers. And all the poets man, thank ya'll for the words, always.

Hope to see ya'll later.
Thank you for reading.